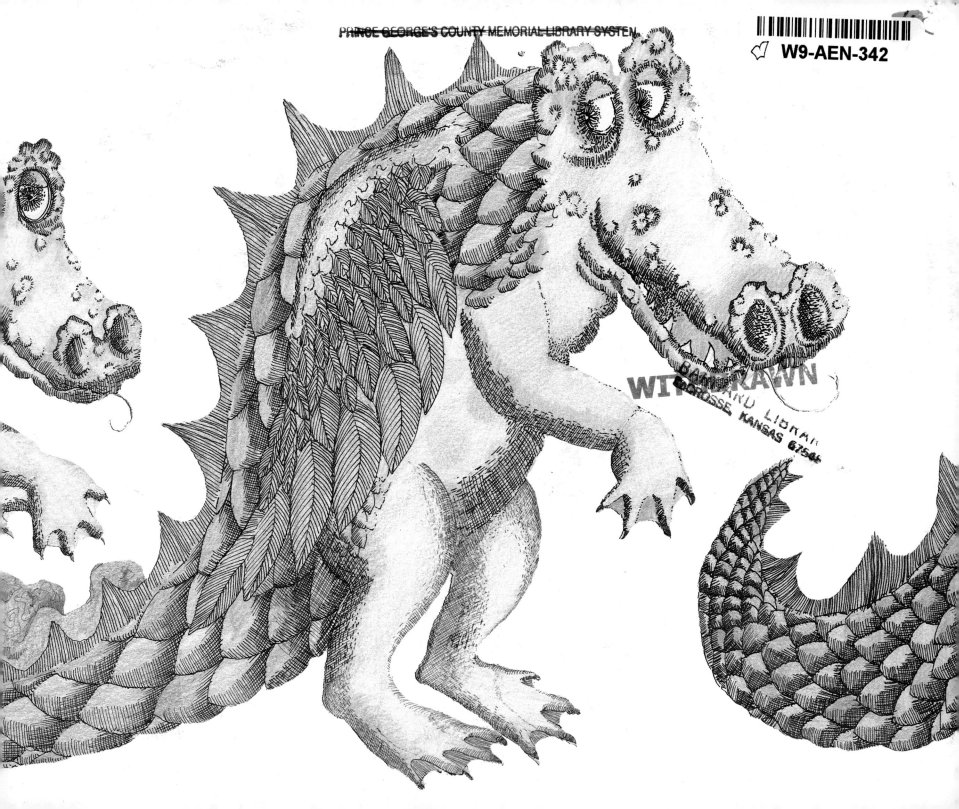

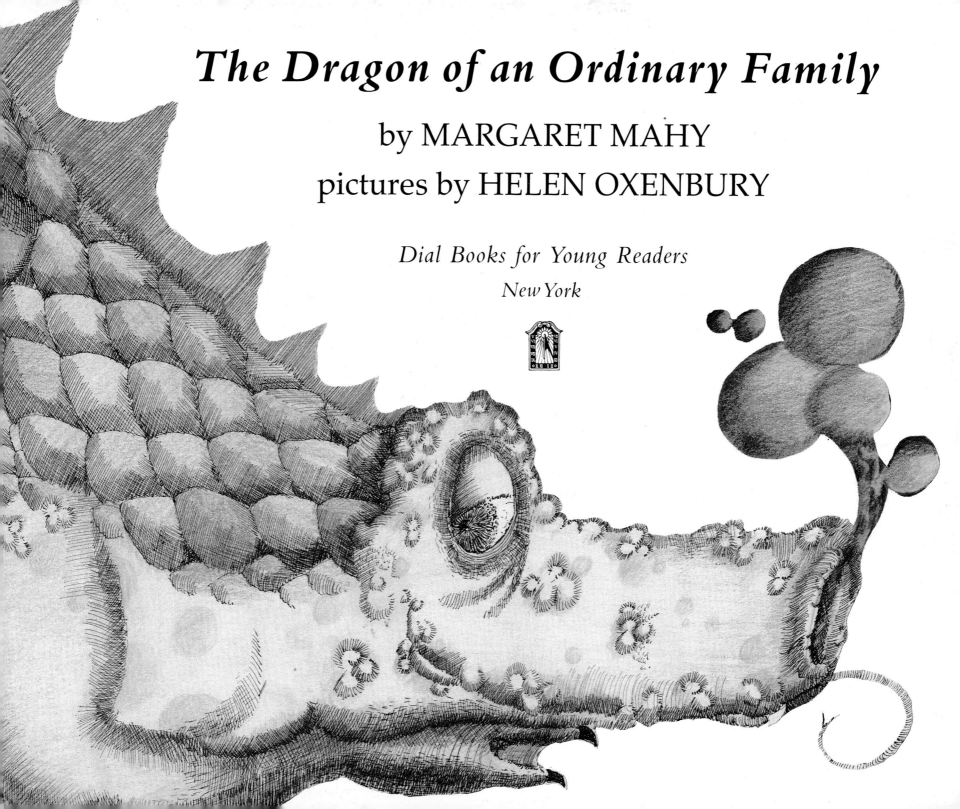

The Dragon of an Ordinary Family

by MARGARET MAHY

pictures by HELEN OXENBURY

Dial Books for Young Readers
New York

First published in the United States 1992
by Dial Books for Young Readers
A Division of Penguin Books USA Inc.
375 Hudson Street • New York, New York 10014

Published in Great Britain 1969, 1991 by William Heinemann Ltd.
Text copyright © 1969, 1991 by Margaret Mahy
Illustrations copyright © 1969 by Helen Oxenbury
Printed in Hong Kong
First Edition
1 3 5 7 9 10 8 6 4 2

Library of Congress Cataloging in Publication Data
Mahy, Margaret.
The dragon of an ordinary family / by Margaret Mahy
pictures by Helen Oxenbury.
p.   cm.
Summary: When Mr. Belsaki chooses a dragon as a pet for
his son, what was a very ordinary family begins
some extraordinary adventures.
ISBN 0-8037-1062-3
1. Dragons—Fiction.   I. Oxenbury, Helen, ill.   II. Title.
PZ7.M2773Dr 1992 [E]—dc20   91-2513   CIP   AC

This edition is a reissue of a 1969 publication, with all art in the same form as in the original edition.

The Dragon of an Ordinary Family

Once there was this family named Belsaki . . . Mr. Belsaki, Mrs. Belsaki, and their little boy, Orlando Belsaki. They were very ordinary people, their house was a very ordinary house on a very ordinary street—and no doubt they would have lived very ordinary lives forever, if one morning Mrs. Belsaki hadn't called Mr. Belsaki a FUDDY-DUDDY.

It was like this:

The day began with breakfast, as usual, with Mr. Belsaki gulping down his hot cereal, a little late for work, as usual. Just as he was rushing out the door, hat and briefcase in hand, Mrs. Belsaki called after him, "On your way home, dear, stop in at the pet shop and buy Orlando a pet."

"A pet!" exclaimed Mr. Belsaki. "What does he want a pet for? We don't have the room, anyway."

"Nonsense!" snapped Mrs. Belsaki. "Of *course* he can have a pet. And we have room for an ELEPHANT, if Orlando wants one."

"An ELEPHANT!" Mr. Belsaki turned slightly pale, and stared in a foolish fashion.

"All right, all right," Mrs. Belsaki said impatiently, "he doesn't *want* an elephant, as it happens. He just wants a puppy—or perhaps a little kitten. . . . Don't be a FUDDY-DUDDY, dear!"

Mr. Belsaki stamped out crossly, pulling his hat down over his ears, muttering, "Fuddy-duddy. Fuddy-duddy, indeed!"

On his way home from work Mr. Belsaki went into the pet shop and looked around. He saw white mice and hamsters, puppies and kittens, all shapes and kinds of birds, some sad-eyed goldfish, and a parrot called Joe, with a sign over him saying NOT FOR SALE.

Mr. Belsaki glowered at them all and glared around the shop.

Then a sign caught his eye. It said UNUSUAL PET, VERY CHEAP. In smaller lettering underneath, it said DRAGON, HOUSE-TRAINED, 50¢.

"That is very reasonable," said Mr. Belsaki to the pet shop man. "I suppose it isn't a very good breed of dragon."

The pet shop man sighed. "No, it's a good breed—the *only* breed," he explained. "But it's a very small one. . . . And not many people want them, you know."

Mr. Belsaki hesitated, and the dragon blinked its violet-blue eyes at him and flicked its tongue out.

"I'll take it!" said Mr. Belsaki loudly.

And that was how it happened that he came home with a tiny dragon in a shoe box.

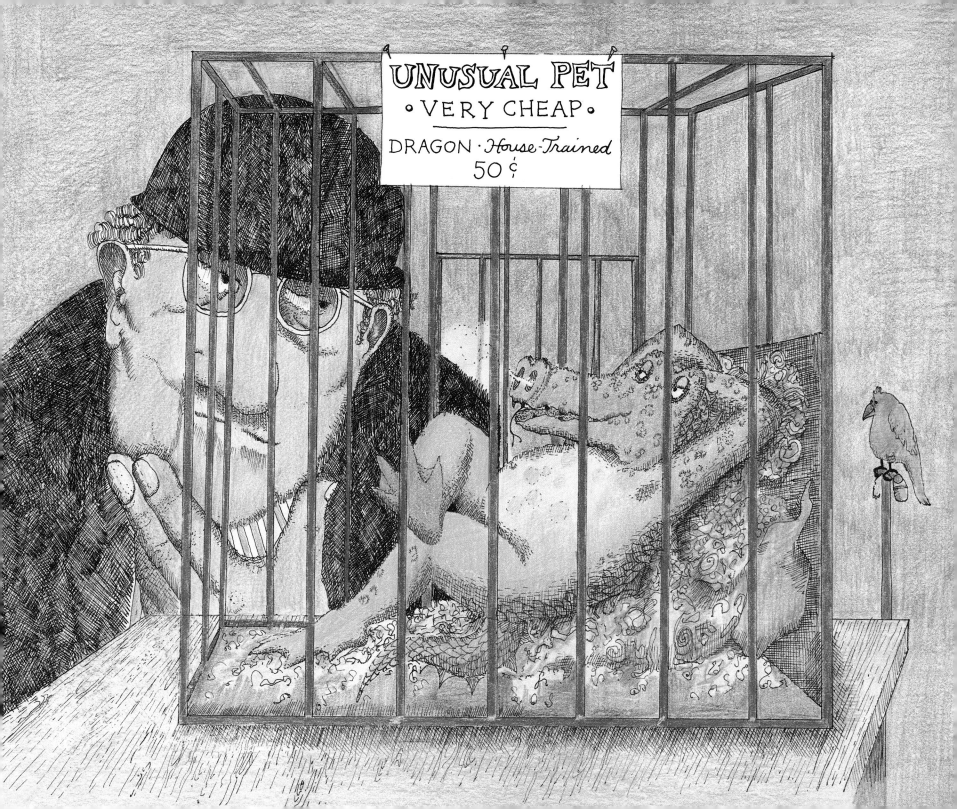

"What on earth is in *there*?" Mrs. Belsaki asked, surprised at the noisy snuffles coming from the shoe box.

"A dragon," replied Mr. Belsaki triumphantly.

"A *dragon*!" Mrs. Belsaki screamed.

"A DRAGON!" cried Orlando in delight.

"It was cheap," Mr. Belsaki answered, clutching the shoe box as if he were afraid that Mrs. Belsaki might snatch it away. "You said I was a FUDDY-DUDDY," he added firmly, "and I am no such thing!"

"You could have chosen something *pretty*," Mrs. Belsaki complained. "A calico kitten perhaps, or a little bird that talks. . . . Where will we *keep* a dragon?"

"We have enough room here to keep an ELEPHANT," Mr. Belsaki reminded her.

So they kept the dragon, and it grew and grew.

It was a wonderful pet for Orlando. He kept it in the shoe box for a while, then in a bird cage, then in a doghouse. He painted a tub for its food, with the word DRAGON on it in red.

The dragon grew and grew. Mrs. Belsaki became very proud of it. "It certainly gives a different look to the place," she said at least once a day. "It makes us a little out of the ordinary."

Her friends said, "What on earth did he get *that* for?" But Mrs. Belsaki would reply, "Because Mr. Belsaki's a man with *ideas*, that's why!" And she always added, "He's not a FUDDY-DUDDY—not like some people."

The dragon grew and grew.
Finally it filled almost the whole yard. It got
so big that it could blow out smoke and fire.

It even got big enough for Orlando to ride.

Then it got as big as an elephant. None of Mrs. Belsaki's friends came to visit anymore. They were afraid.

The dragon grew. . . .

It grew *bigger* than an elephant!

It grew TOO big!

One day the Mayor came to look at the Belsakis' dragon. He studied it and studied it.

"It is *much* too big to keep in this town," he said crossly. "Mr. Belsaki, you have just an ordinary family, and you should stick to ordinary pets. Mr. Belsaki, you must sell it . . . to a zoo. Or to a circus . . . Or to a handbag factory. Some people would pay a lot for dragon skin."

Mr. and Mrs. Belsaki looked very worried and sad. They loved their dragon, but, beyond all doubt, it *was* growing too big. Besides, it cost so much to feed. And winter was coming.

"We can't even afford to buy a Christmas tree, or go for a vacation this year," Mr. Belsaki said gloomily.

"Well, *I* would rather have our dragon!" Orlando cried.

"Well, you can't," the Mayor answered snappishly. "It is just too much! You have exactly one week to get rid of it."

And he marched away.

"As if we would sell our dragon!" Mrs. Belsaki said indignantly. "And we certainly don't want him made into a handbag! Oh, if only we knew of a dragon-loving farmer. We could give him away to a really good farmer."

Then the dragon turned around and faced them. For the first time, he spoke. "As a matter of fact, it *is* getting a little cramped here for me. Though I am fond of you all, I feel that I should move someplace else. How would you like to come with *me* for the Christmas holidays?"

"Where were you thinking of going?" Mr. Belsaki asked cautiously.

"To the Isles of Magic," the dragon answered. "*All* dragons know the way there."

Mrs. Belsaki thought a moment. "Well, that *might* be all right. I'll go and pack."

So the Mayor, and Mrs. Belsaki's friends, and all their ordinary neighbors were amazed to see Mr. and Mrs. Belsaki and Orlando Belsaki soon fly away on the dragon's back—off for the holidays—with their suitcases and shopping bags and baskets and boxes tied to the dragon's tail.

Higher and higher the dragon flew—way up into the clouds—and then, after a long time, he dropped down, down, down. And there, below them, lay the bluest-blue sea, with the Isles of Magic spread across it, all gold and green as if summer leaves had been blown there by a dreaming wind.

Oh, the Isles of Magic!

But what would the Belsakis do on the Isles of Magic? The dragon explained to them as they flew along that the Isles of Magic are the homes of all the wonderful, strange, fairy-tale people. So what would an ordinary family from an ordinary home on an ordinary street in an ordinary town—what would *they* do on the Isles of Magic?

This is what the Belsakis did:

They walked in the forests, the green and gold, the dark and old forests. They saw the starry towers of castles rising above the trees, and princesses sitting in windows combing their hair. They met all kinds of sons—the youngest sons of kings, of millers, of cobblers, and of beggars—all seeking fortunes.

Some days they went sailing in a huge galleon over shining seas, diving for pearls through deep, green water. They hunted and sailed with pirates, and buried treasure in golden sand on islands where parrots screamed and monkeys mocked in the palm trees. And all the while the Belsakis could hear mermaids singing among the great, black rocks under the lacy veil of the spray.

On other days they searched for lost cities in twining jungles—and found them, too!—cities of ivory, cities of gold, forgotten and terribly old. . . . Or they watched witches twitch their broomsticks over the sky.

On the far horizon, like mountains, giants moved on their mysterious business. From the windows of the castle they lived in, the Belsaki family watched them curiously and nervously—and kept their distance.

When Christmas came, they sang their carols around a tree covered in small candles accommodatingly formed by hundreds of fireflies—a tree so high that a real star shivered, fragile and far, on its top.

Mr. Belsaki's best present was a special pipe that played strange, wild music. Mrs. Belsaki got a sewing basket set with emeralds, with an ivory thimble and little silver scissors shaped like a stork. Orlando got a chess set where little knights and queens and pawns came alive and chased one another all over the board.

At last the time came for them to go back home. The dragon stayed, for the Isles of Magic are the best place for dragons.

The Belsaki family sailed off for home on a flying carpet, and as a farewell present, the dragon gave Orlando a tiny black kitten with an oversized purr.

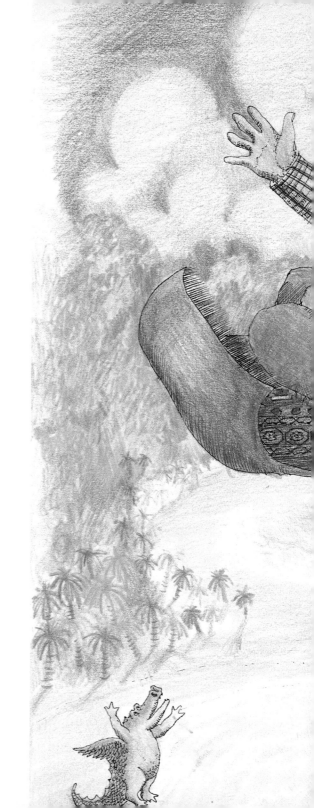

"Now," said Mrs. Belsaki, as she looked lovingly around her kitchen, "we can settle down to be nice, ordinary people again. I'm very glad Mr. Belsaki is *not* a FUDDY-DUDDY, and I *was* very fond of that dragon—but I must say it will be pleasant to relax with our neighbors again."

"Next Christmas," Orlando asked hopefully, "can we visit the Isles of Magic and see our dragon?"

"Who knows," said Mrs. Belsaki, a little wistfully, "we may *never see* him again. . . ." Then she said, a little sadly, "I suppose we'll just have to settle down and *be* an ordinary family. Perhaps no other magic will ever happen to us again."

Suddenly the little black kitten awoke and sat up tall in Orlando's lap. "I wouldn't be too sure of that," he murmured, and went back to sleep.